A TURNER PICTURES WORLDWIDE RELEASE
TURNER ENTERTAINMENT CO. IN ASSOCIATION WITH WMG PRESENTS A FILM ROMAN PRODUCTION
"TOM AND JERRY -- THE MOVIE" SCREENPLAY BY DENNIS MARKS SONGS BY HENRY MANCINI & LESLIE BRICUSSE
MUSICAL SCORE BY HENRY MANCINI MUSIC SUPERVISED BY SHARON BOYLE
EXECUTIVE PRODUCERS ROGER MAYER JACK PETRIK HANS BROCKMANN JUSTIN ACKERMAN
CREATIVE CONSULTANT JOSEPH BARBERA PRODUCED AND DIRECTED BY PHIL ROMAN

Original Motion Picture Soundtrack Album on MCA Compact Discs and Cassettes   © 1993 TURNER ENTERTAINMENT CO. AND TELEFILM-ESSEN GMBH

Adapted by Jordan Horowitz
From the screenplay by Dennis Marks

Book Design by Elizabeth B. Parisi

ISBN 0-590-47116-3

12 11 10 9 8 7 6 5 4 3 2   3 4 5 6 7 8/9

Printed in the U.S.A.   24
First Scholastic printing, July 1993

SCHOLASTIC INC.
New York Toronto London Auckland Sydney

It was moving day for Tom.

All the houses in his neighborhood were going to be knocked down. They would be replaced with tall apartment buildings. Most of the neighbors had already moved away.

Now everything in Tom's house was being loaded into a large moving van.

On that day, Tom was busy concentrating on some very important cat business. He was sleeping under the couch! In fact, Tom was so busy sleeping he didn't even notice that the movers had taken the couch!

"Thomas!" He heard his owner calling. "Hurry up, Tom! We're leaving!"

Tom instantly woke up at the sound of his name and saw that the couch was gone!

He quickly grabbed up all of his belongings—a food dish and a big fluffy pillow. Then he sped out of the house and leaped into the back of the family station wagon.

Jerry lived in a little hole in the wall.

When he saw that Tom had already packed up and gone, Jerry took his satchel and blanket and ran out after him. He didn't want to be left behind.

Climbing into the back of the station wagon, Jerry spread out his blanket and prepared for the long trip to his new home.

But Tom did not want Jerry to come along. He was tired of being bothered by the pesky mouse. All they ever did was fight. So Tom lifted Jerry up on the end of a pool cue and threw him out of the car.

But Jerry was too smart for Tom. He grabbed onto the cat's long whiskers.

S-T-R-E-T-C-H! went Tom's whiskers.

Tom and Jerry went flying out of the car together! *THUMPETY-THUMP!* They landed on the sidewalk.

Jerry got up and ran over Tom's head, bouncing across his nose as he went.

He ran all the way to the house and back into his mouse hole.

BANG! BANG! POUND! WHAM! Jerry heard a loud noise while he was inside his hole.

Tom was covering his hole with boards and nails!

Tom grinned happily. Now that mouse would never bother him again!

Tom went back out to the street, but by the time he got there the station wagon had gone. Tom had been left behind!

That night, Tom slept in the big, empty house. It was very lonely.

The next morning he was awakened by a loud crash.

CRASH! SMASH! WHAM! A wrecking ball broke through the wall.

Outside, construction workers were tearing down the house.

Tom ran out of the house as fast as he could.

Then Tom remembered that Jerry was still trapped inside the mouse hole!

If anything happened to Jerry, who would Tom have to fight with?

So Tom ran all the way back into the house and rescued Jerry from the mouse hole.

Then Tom and Jerry fled from the house together.

From the street they saw their house crumble to the ground.

Tom and Jerry were very sad. They had no home to go back to anymore.

So they decided to visit the big city. It was a long trip and they soon became hungry. Along the way they spotted a restaurant. The window was filled with many pictures of delicious foods.

But when Tom went in to get something to eat, he was thrown back out on the sidewalk. *FLUMP! FLUMP! FLUMP!*

Tom decided it would be better if he and Jerry went their separate ways.

But every time Tom started to walk away, Jerry followed.

So Tom stuffed Jerry under a flower pot.

"Well, well, well," he heard someone say. "Look at the big brave pussycat!"

"Yeah," said someone else. "Pickin' on a poor little teensy-weensy mouse!"

When Tom turned around, he saw that a dog was watching him from the seat of an old beat-up jalopy.

"First time out, eh?" said the dog. "And instead of bein' pals, you're fightin' like cat and mouse."

"Dey *are* a cat anna mouse, Puggsy," came the other voice.

Now Tom was confused. He could see the dog, but where was the other voice coming from?

Then he looked closer. There was a speck moving on the dog's nose. But it wasn't a speck at all. It was a tiny flea!

"Frankie Da Flea is the name," said the flea. "I'm of French extraction."

"The name's Puggsy," said the dog. "What's yours?"

"I'm Tom," said Tom.

"I'm Jerry," said Jerry.

Tom looked down. Jerry had escaped from under the flower pot!
Tom was very annoyed. He wanted to slap Jerry, but Puggsy
stopped him.

"I told you before," he told Tom and Jerry. "You guys gotta learn
to be friends."

"A cat and a mouse? Friends?" said Tom. "That's disgusting!
No way!"

"That goes double for me!" said Jerry.

Tom and Jerry left Puggsy and Frankie Da Flea and wandered to the riverfront. They were still looking for food.

Suddenly a big shadow fell over them.

Was it a mean bulldog?

Was it an angry alley cat?

No! It was a little girl named Robyn Starling. She had run away from home and she was very, very sad.

"Who...who are you?" asked Robyn.

"He's Tom and I'm Jerry," said the mouse. "We're lost and we're looking for something to eat. We're kind of hungry."

"Well, let me see," said Robyn. She reached inside her knapsack and pulled out some apples and some cookies.

The cookies were as big as Jerry!

Soon everybody's tummies were stuffed with food.

"I'm an orphan," explained Robyn when they had finished eating all the cookies. "My father was climbing a mountain when the snow gave way in a–a–"

"An avalanche?" asked Tom.

"Uh-huh," said Robyn. Now she had to live with her mean old Aunt Figg.

"Aunt Figg has taken over the house," said Robyn. "She locked me in the attic and gave my room to her dog Ferdinand!"

Both Tom and Jerry knew how important it was to have a home. They convinced Robyn that she should go back and give Aunt Figg a second chance.

But as soon as Robyn went back home, Aunt Figg locked her in the attic again. "You're going to bed without dinner," Aunt Figg said. Next she called The Straycatchers to come and take Tom and Jerry away. "We really don't have enough room for them here, do we?" she asked.

Just then, Aunt Figg got an urgent telegram from Lickboot, her crooked lawyer. Robyn's father was still alive! That meant Aunt Figg would not be able to use his money anymore. "Robyn must never know," Aunt Figg told Lickboot.

Tom and Jerry had heard everything. They had to tell Robyn that her father was safe.

But before they could find her, Aunt Figg grabbed hold of Tom. "Oh, no, you don't!" she said, pulling Tom's tail. Tom's legs were running, but he wasn't getting anywhere at all.

Jerry tried to escape. He ran all the way down the hall...and right into a jar! Ferdinand had trapped him!

The Straycatchers came and took Tom and Jerry to Dr. Applecheek's house.

Dr. Applecheek was a mean animal doctor. He kidnapped cats and dogs and sold them for money. Dr. Applecheek put Tom and Jerry in a cage in the basement.

"Well, well, well!" Tom and Jerry heard a familiar voice say.

They looked into the next cage. It was Puggsy and Frankie Da Flea!

"The Straycatchers finally got me," said Puggsy. "So I ain't so perfect all the time."

"I been tellin' ya that for years," Frankie agreed.

When Tom and Jerry explained that little Robyn Starling was in trouble, everyone agreed they had to escape and help her.

Later that night, Tom and Jerry saw that The Straycatchers had fallen asleep at the controls. This was their chance.

Since Frankie Da Flea was so small, he was able to jump through the bars on his cage. He ran over to the controls and tried to press the biggest button. He pushed and he pressed and he squeezed and he huffed. Finally he rolled up his sleeves, leaped in the air, and landed with both feet on the button.

All the animal cages opened at once.

"All right," said Puggsy. *"Everybody out!"*

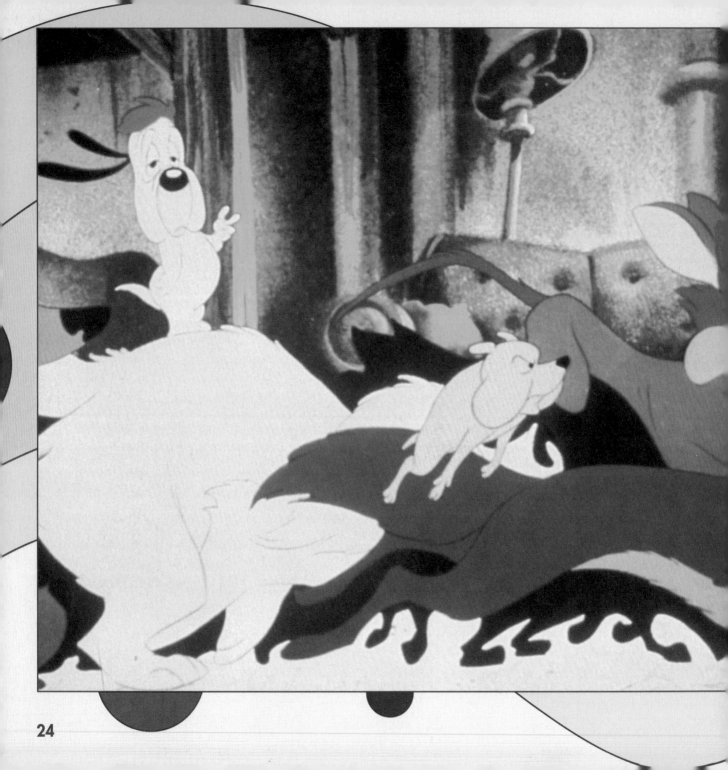

BARK! BARK! MEOW! YOWL! All the cats and dogs fled from their cages. They were free!

Tom and Jerry ran straight back to Robyn's house.

"Robyn, have we got news for you!" said Jerry.

When Robyn heard that her father was still alive she wanted to find him. So she made a long rope from the bedsheet and climbed out the window.

Tom and Jerry followed. They were going to help Robyn find her father.

The three friends ran down to the river. There they boarded an old crate. Soon Robyn, Tom, and Jerry were floating down the river on the crate.

It was foggy and they couldn't see where they were going. Suddenly they crashed into a fishing schooner! *R-I-I-I-I-P-P-P!* Their crate split in two.

Tom and Jerry drifted one way down the river.

Robyn drifted the other.

Robyn was rescued by a man named Captain Kiddie and his parrot puppet Squawk. They lived in the carnival park.

But Aunt Figg had offered a million-dollar reward for Robyn.

"I'm rich! I'm rich!" said Captain Kiddie gleefully when he saw Robyn's picture on a milk carton.

"What do you mean you're rich?" asked Squawk. "We're both rich!"

"Oh, yeah," said Captain Kiddie. "I forgot."

First the Captain called Aunt Figg. Then he trapped Robyn on top of a Ferris wheel so she could not run away.

Aunt Figg and Lickboot took off in their sports car. They were going to the carnival park to get Robyn. Ferdinand jumped into the back seat. He did not want to be left out.

When Dr. Applecheek found out where Robyn was, he wanted the million-dollar reward too. So he and his Straycatchers drove off to the carnival in their van.

Along the way they got into an argument and The Straycatchers threw Dr. Applecheek out of the van. He spied an ice cream cart and hopped on.

Now everybody was looking for Robyn Starling!

When Tom and Jerry got to the park, they saw that Robyn was trapped at the top of the Ferris wheel.

Captain Kiddie was guarding the Ferris wheel. But he was fast asleep!

Tom and Jerry came up with a plan. Tom held a fishing pole over the controls. He lowered the fish hook right next to Captain Kiddie's feet. Jerry slipped the fish hook around the control switch while Tom reeled it in. CLICK! The Ferris wheel began to turn!

Tom and Jerry rescued Robyn from the Ferris wheel. Then they helped her escape in Captain Kiddie's paddle wheeler.

As the paddle wheeler pulled away from shore, Captain Kiddie and Squawk chased them in a small motorboat.

The Straycatchers chased them in the animal van.

Dr. Applecheek chased them in the ice cream cart.

Aunt Figg and Lickboot chased them in the sports car.

Aunt Figg's car roared across a rickety wooden bridge. The bridge broke in half behind her!

Dr. Applecheek followed her across the bridge but he didn't see that the bridge was out until it was too late. His cart fell through the hole and crashed right on top of Captain Kiddie and Squawk in their motorboat! *SPLAT!*

Robyn, Tom, and Jerry were safe in the paddle wheeler. So they headed down the river to Robyn's cabin in the woods. "Daddy will know where to find me," Robyn told Tom and Jerry.

"If you know what's good for you, you'll never run away again," they heard someone say. It was Aunt Figg! She had found them.

"You'll never take me back!" said Robyn, kicking Lickboot in the shin.

Lickboot jumped up and down holding his leg in pain. But as he hopped around he bumped into the table and knocked his lantern on the floor.

Suddenly the cabin caught fire!

Aunt Figg, Lickboot, and Ferdinand ran out of the cabin. They did not care about anybody but themselves.

Robyn was still trapped inside the house. A fallen rafter blocked her way.

Tom and Jerry raced to the skylight and threw a rope down to Robyn. She climbed the rope and crawled out onto the roof.

Suddenly she heard the sound of a helicopter. It was Daddy Starling! He had come to rescue her!

"Oh, Daddy, I knew you'd come," said Robyn as soon as she was in her father's arms.

"You're safe now, Robyn," said Daddy Starling. "I'm here."

When Robyn reached back to rescue her two friends, they were nowhere in sight. The burning cabin had collapsed into the water. "Tom! Jerry!" screamed Robyn.

All at once the cat and mouse popped up out of the water. Tom and Jerry were alive!

Now, Tom and Jerry still needed a place to live. So they moved into the Starling mansion with Robyn and her father. Tom had a new bed and Jerry had a newly furnished mouse hole.

Tom waited for Jerry to move into the new mouse hole. Then he stuffed it with a brand new mousetrap!

Jerry escaped through a secret back entrance and tied the mousetrap to Tom's tail.

SNAP! Tom's tail got caught in the mousetrap!

Tom and Jerry were very happy once again.